MARY AND THE WITCH'S SECRET

MARY AND THE WITCH'S SECRET

CATHY LESURF

ILLUSTRATED BY
PETER KAVANAGH

ORCHARD BOOKS

ORCHARD BOOKS
96 Leonard Street, London EC2A 4RH

Orchard Books Australia
14 Mars Road, Lane Cove, NSW 2066
ISBN 1 85213 511 5 (paperback)
ISBN 1 85213 162 4 (hardback)

First published in Great Britain 1989
as MARY AND THE TEN LITTLE BROTHERS AND SISTERS
First paperback publication 1993
Text copyright © Cathy Lesurf 1989
Illustrations copyright © Peter Kavanagh 1993

Printed and bound by The Guernsey Press, Channel Islands
A CIP catalogue record for this book is available from the British Library.

For Katie Stuart,
our Nanna Sallows,
who left me
a precious legacy
of stories and
of music.

1

Just outside the town, on the edge of the great forest, lived the woodman and his family. Mary was the eldest child and she had ten little brothers and sisters. They all lived in a very small cottage and they were very poor.

All the little sisters had to sleep in one bed, top-to-toe, and all the little brothers slept in another. It was a tight squeeze to fit them all in.

If someone rolled over in the bed, all the others had to roll over, too, and the one on the end would roll over the edge and fall out of bed onto the floor. It also wasn't very nice to wake up in the middle of the night with someone's toe up your nose.

Mary helped her mother
look after the ten little
brothers and sisters.
On market day they all
helped their father carry
bundles of firewood
to sell in the market square.

One night, when all the little brothers and sisters had gone hungry to bed, and there was no more food in the house, Mary's mother said:

"Tomorrow is a very special market day, Mary, my dear. There will be a hiring fair. All the people who want work will go, and all the people who want workers will go to hire them.

"You must go, too, and get a job as a servant to some fine lady, for there is no more food and no more money left. When you are asked what you can do, say you can clean and sew and do plain cooking. Say, you'll work hard, and that you'd like sixpence a week."

Mary got up
before the sun
the next morning,
and dressed in the dark.
One of the little sisters was snoring, and
one of the little brothers had been pushed
out of bed and was asleep on the floor with
his mouth wide open. Mary kissed her
mother and set off for market – and the
hiring fair.

She arrived in the cobbled square in the grey, early light, while the traders were setting out their wares. There was Mary's friend, the apple-seller.

She was a wide, plump old lady, who always wore a black dress and a big white apron. She reached into the deep pocket of this apron and fished out her breakfast to share with Mary: bread, cheese and apples.

"Do you see those
three men by the
ginger-bread stall,
carrying garden rakes?"
asked the apple-seller.
"They're gardeners,
looking for work.

See those two women,
one of them's holding
a wooden spoon,
and the other's
got a rolling pin?
They're cooks.
I know the one
with the spoon –
she's that sour-faced,
she could curdle milk!"

Just then, the first of the crowd began to arrive, coming from the town, and from the villages, farms and fine houses.

"You'd better go and stand with the other little servant-girls," said the apple-seller. "And good luck!"

The sun rose higher. The market square grew more and more crowded. The traders shouted and sang about their wares to attract customers. Many of the workers at the hiring fair were offered jobs and drifted away, but no one spoke to Mary.

The farmers' wives looked her up and down, and decided she was too thin; not strong enough to help in the farmhouse. The fine ladies turned up their noses at her ragged clothes and rough hands.

Mary thought of the ten
little brothers and sisters,
with their hungry faces,
and stood there patiently.
More and more people
left, until she was the
only little servant-girl
standing in the square.
She couldn't bear to go
home without a job.

16

Suddenly, the traders fell silent and the birds stopped singing. The last customers hurried away, as if they sensed a thunderstorm coming.

A thin figure swept into the square, her clothes billowing like a dark cloud around her. She didn't know why, but Mary felt she wanted to run away, only her feet wouldn't move.

The figure was coming closer.
In the tense stillness,
a black crow flew lazily
up into the air and
settled on the
tallest tree to watch.
The hair on the back
of Mary's neck prickled,
and she remembered
the whispered stories
about the witch
of the forest.

Suddenly
Mary knew
that in front
of her stood
the wicked witch.

"Not much flesh on you, is there?" said the witch, pinching Mary's arm with bony fingers.

"Skinny as a rat!" she said, pinching Mary's cheek hard. Mary felt like a joint of meat being tested for the dinner table.

"So you want a job, do you, girl?" asked the witch, staring nastily into Mary's eyes.

Mary wanted to say no, but she was a brave girl who didn't run away from things, so she repeated what her mother had told her.

"Yes, ma'am. I can clean and sew and do plain cooking. I'll work very hard, and I'd like sixpence a week."

"Sixpence a week!" shrieked the witch, who was known to be mean. "You can have threepence a week, or sixpence a fortnight. It's all you're worth."

"If you please, ma'am," replied Mary, thinking that her mother must know best, "my mother says I'm to have sixpence."

The witch glared at Mary, and in the silence, the little girl's stomach seemed to her to float up into her throat, down into her boots, turn a somersault and tie itself in a knot. She was brave, but that didn't mean she wasn't frightened.

Then the witch, quick as lightning, smacked Mary on the ear with a fist like a bag of nails and said, "Very well, but don't think you can get the better of me."

As the witch led
the way out of
the market square,
the apple-seller
watched them go.
"I wouldn't like
a child of mine
to work for that
old crow," she said.

And the big black crow, sitting in the
tallest tree, looked very offended and flew
off.

2

The wicked witch led Mary deep into the forest. At first it was very pleasant, with sunlight flooding through the leaves and the ground soft under foot. But after a while, the trees seemed darker and more secretive, as if they were crowding together to whisper nasty things.

Mary felt as if someone were staring at her, and even spun round once to see who was there. No one was. Only the trees.

It was dark when they reached the witch's cottage. The witch lit a lamp in the kitchen, the warm yellow glow showing up enough dirt for an army of little servant-girls to clean. The floor felt strangely lumpy under foot, although the uneven stones were covered by a thick rush mat.

The witch said, "I'll have my breakfast in bed in the morning. Make sure the eggs are just right, not too runny and not too hard, and the porridge isn't too lumpy, and the toast is still warm. You can sleep on that bench."

And without so much as a 'goodnight', the witch went to bed, taking the lamp with her.

Waking with the sun
the next morning,
Mary was so
uncomfortable on
the wooden bench,
she was glad
to get up.

She went outside and
found a water pump
and a bucket.
There were hens
scratching in the garden,
but no birds sang
close to the cottage.
No flowers grew for the
wicked witch, but only
bold stinging nettles.

After fetching the water, Mary began the enormous task of cleaning the kitchen. She had just reached the biggest pile of washing up she had ever seen, when the witch called out, "Mary! Wretched girl! Where's my breakfast? I said I wanted breakfast in bed – not lunch in bed!"

Mary found bread and porridge oats, but the eggs were a more difficult matter. The hens didn't like the witch, and laid their eggs in the most out-of-the-way places to stop her finding them. But Mary scattered some crumbs and made friends with them, and under the hedge she found three eggs.

Then she cooked the witch's breakfast, and kept her fingers crossed that everything would be done just right.

When Mary carried in the breakfast tray, the witch was sitting up in bed, wearing a greasy nightcap. She stuffed the food into her mouth as fast as she could, and all at once: eggs, marmalade, porridge and toast together.

With a very runny mouthful, she said, "While you're cleaning, remember these three things:

"Don't lift up the kitchen carpet;
Don't lift up the tablecoth;
And don't open the cupboard
under the sink.
For if you do, I'll break your bones,
And lay you under cold marble stones!"

It was just the sort of horrible thing the witch would say, but Mary was pleased to have three fewer jobs to do.

31

Dear Mother and Father
. I am writing to you
from the wicked witch's
cottage. She is quite
strange and scary but she
has given me a job and is
paying me sixpence a week.
Here is the first sixpence
with this letter—it should help
pay for some food. I miss
you all so much.
Love from Mary. X

In those days, posting letters wasn't as easy as it is today, even for those people who could write. It took a long time for Mary to write a letter, and even longer to get her wages from the witch, who had to be asked at least three times.

But Mary wrote to her family every week, and wrapped her sixpences up in the letters. When the witch went to market, Mary asked her to give the letter to the apple-seller who would pass it on to Mary's family.

At least that's what Mary thought, until the day the apple-seller arrived at the witch's cottage.

The witch had gone to market that day, saying, as usual:

"Don't look under the carpet;
And don't look under the tablecloth;
And don't look in the cupboard
under the sink.
For if you do, I'll break your bones,
And lay you under cold marble stones."

As soon as she had disappeared into the forest, the apple-seller knocked on the cottage door. She had bad news.

"My daughter, Amy, is minding the stall at market, today," she said. "I promised your mother and father that I'd find out what had become of you. We've all been very worried. All these weeks you've been gone, and we haven't had one letter from you."

Mary couldn't believe her ears. "I've been sending letters, and my wages, with the witch to you on market days. Has none of them arrived?"

"None," said the apple-seller. "Oh, Mary, come away with me now. I can't bear to think of you here with the wicked witch."

"But then I'll have no money to take home, and things will be just as bad as before," Mary replied, being brave and stubborn – which is sometimes a good thing, and sometimes not. "I'll have to stay and think of a plan to outwit the witch."

The witch didn't like to have her clothes washed, but when her cloaks got too muddy and dusty, she told Mary to hang them on the washing-line and beat the dust out of them with the carpet beater. The market day after the apple-seller's visit was a cloak-beating day.

Mary pretended the cloak on the washing-line was the witch. "Take THAT! And THAT!" she was shouting. "I'll give you:

"Don't look under the carpet;

WHACK!

And don't look under
the tablecloth;

THWACK!

And don't look in the cupboard
under the sink.

THUMP!

So you'll break my bones, will you?
And lay me under cold marble stones, hey?"

38

Then Mary stopped
and thought, "What is
under the carpet, and
under the tablecloth
and in the cupboard?
I'm going to find out,
before the witch
comes back from market!"

Inside the cottage, everything
was perfectly quiet.
Mary lifted the edge
of the old rush mat
in the kitchen, and
looked underneath.
Nothing.
She lifted the mat
a little more.

The stone floor was hollowed out in the middle, and lying under the mat was a fortune in golden money.

She looked under the tablecloth – more golden money. She looked in the cupboard under the sink – boxes and boxes of golden money.

Mary remembered the witch's threat and was afraid. But then she thought of the little brothers and sisters and their hungry faces. So she fetched a basket and filled it with gold. She filled her apron, and even her socks, with as much money as she could carry, enough to keep her family from hunger for ever.

Then she fled into the forest.

3

In the market square, the witch took Mary's sixpence out of the letter and put it in her pocket. As she tore the letter into tiny pieces and threw it away, she suddenly felt a shadow pass over her heart.

She let out a howl, as in her mind's eye she saw Mary running through the forest with her golden money. The witch ran into the forest, and gave chase.

And where was Mary? She was running as fast as she could, stumbling over roots and fallen branches. Her arms soon began to ache with the weight of the gold. Her legs ached.

She ran on and on, until she could run no more. Mary needed somewhere to hide. Close by, she saw a huge hollow tree and said:

"Oak tree, oak tree, hide me,
In case the old witch finds me.
For if she do, she'll break my bones,
And lay me under cold marble stones!"

There was a sound in the tree, which might have been the breeze blowing through the branches, and Mary heard a voice, so soft it might have been her own thoughts: "I'm sorry, little girl, but the witch will find you here."

So, Mary ran on.

And where was the witch?
She was getting closer and closer.

The witch was
running
as fast as
the wind,

and she
could smell
the golden
money.

Mary ran until she was so tired, her feet were dragging the ground. She ran until she tripped and fell, and lay on the forest floor, smelling the damp earth and leaves and moss. As she lifted her weary head, she found herself staring into the entrance of a badger's set. She said:

"Badger, badger, hide me,
In case the old witch finds me.
For if she do, she'll break my bones,
And lay me under cold marble stones."

From inside the shadowy
hole, there came a rustle,
and Mary heard a voice,
so soft it might have
been her own thoughts:
"I'm sorry, little girl, but
the witch will find you here."

Mary climbed to her feet,
her legs like jelly, and ran on.

And the witch was getting closer all the
time.

Suddenly, Mary ran out of the trees and into a clearing. Ahead, she saw the glint of water in the sun. It was the river that ran through the town and through the great forest and on to the sea.

In the middle of the clearing stood a man wearing a white apron. His arms were buried in a mound of bread dough. It was the baker.

He looked up in surprise as the little girl came stumbling out of the forest with big, frightened eyes, and covered in scratches and dirt. But before he could speak, Mary said:

"Baker, baker, hide me
In case the old witch finds me.
For if she do, she'll break my bones,
And lay me under cold marble stones."

"Why?" asked the baker. "Whatever have you done?"

"I promise I haven't done anything bad," wailed Mary, looking over her shoulder in case the witch came bursting out of the forest.

"I was working for the wicked witch. She was so cruel to me, and then she stole all my wages that should have fed my family.

"So, I took some of her golden money, so that the little brothers and sisters will never be hungry again, but if she catches me! Oh, baker! Please hide me, for she said she'd break my bones and lay me under cold marble stones!"

The baker could see how tired and ter-rified the little girl was. He had heard the stories about the wicked witch, and didn't like the look of her himself, but he knew that you mustn't always believe all the bad things people say about each other.

"I'll hide you," he said, "and get you back safe to your family. But to satisfy the witch and stop her chasing you, I'll give her back the basket of gold.

"I'll say you dropped it as you ran, and that I last saw you swimming across the river. A witch can't cross running water, you know, so when she gets her money back, I'm sure she'll leave you alone."

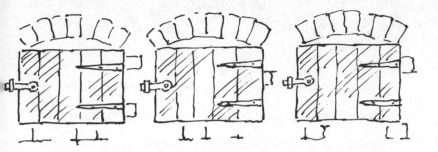

The baker had three ovens. One of them was full of baking bread. The second one was heating up, and the third one would not be lit that day. In this cold oven, Mary hid.

In the darkness, with aching legs and pounding heart, Mary listened and waited. She heard the birds singing, and the baker humming to himself to keep his courage up. Then there was silence, and she knew the witch had arrived.

"Where is she?" screamed the witch, shaking her fist under the baker's nose. "I know she's here. I know my money's here. Where are you hiding that wicked girl, Mary?"

"I don't know any wicked girls,"
replied the baker, coldly.
"A little girl ran past
a while ago, and swam
across the river. She
dropped a basket as
she ran, and if you
say it's yours,
you're welcome to
take it back."

"I'll take my basket back,
all right, but I'll have
Mary, too. Do you know
what I can do to you,
if you don't tell me
where she's hiding?"

55

The witch listed a number of horrid spells. When she threatened to turn him into a slug and eat him in a sandwich with sauce, the baker had had enough.

"If you're so sure she's here," he said, "why don't you look for yourself?"

Inside the dark oven, Mary began to tremble. Would the baker betray her? Footsteps approached.

They went straight to the basket of gold, behind the first oven. The witch flung open that oven door to see if Mary was inside.

"Now you've got your gold back," said the baker, "why don't you just forget the little girl? Let her go."

"I know you've got her hidden here, and I'm going to break her bones and lay her under cold marble stones," said the witch cruelly.

She opened the door of the second oven, which was now hot. The baker knew there was only one way to save the little girl, and to save himself.

With a great shove, he pushed the witch inside the second oven and shut the door. In a puff of raging smoke, she disappeared, and was never seen in that place again.

Mary rode home in
the baker's cart.
When they got to
the woodman's
cottage,

all the little brothers
and sisters rushed
outside and shouted
with excitement at
seeing Mary again –
and not just Mary
but also the baker
and the baker's horse!

Inside the cottage, Mary tipped out the golden money in a glittering shower onto the floor.

When Mary's father and mother realised that she was safe, and that they would never go hungry again, they laughed and cried for joy.

Everyone was dancing
and hugging and
singing and shouting.
Then Mary gave the
baker a bag of gold
for his goodness
and bravery.

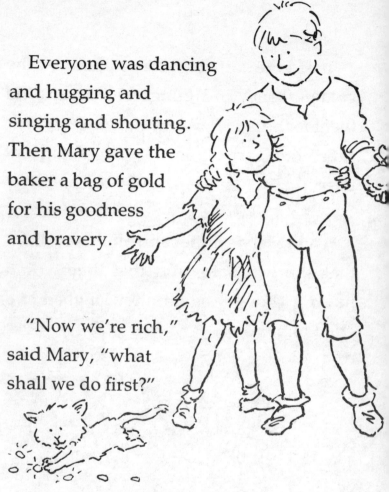

"Now we're rich,"
said Mary, "what
shall we do first?"

All the little brothers and sisters shouted
at once, but Mother said that Mary should
choose. So she did.

That evening, they all put on the new clothes Mary had bought for them and went to the fair. It was not a hiring fair, this time, but a fun fair. They had a go at everything.

There was a dance tent, where a real band was playing, and Mary, her parents, and the ten little brothers and sisters danced all night.

When the story of the witch's gold got round the town, many people went into the forest to look for the cottage. Strangely, though, it was never found again. Soon the path to the witch's cottage disappeared and people forgot about her.

Only the kind apple-seller remembered the whole adventure and she told the story many times to the children in the town. She went to live with Mary's family in their beautiful, new house. And in comfort and togetherness, they all lived happily for the rest of their lives.